Christopher Fowler is the acclaimed author of eleven novels, including *Roofworld*, *Spanky*, *Psychoville* and *Soho Black*, and nine collections of short stories including *City Jitters*, *Sharper Knives*, *Uncut* and *The Devil In Me*. He is a director of the film marketing company Creative Partnership, and lives in London.

Also by Christopher Fowler

Novels

ROOFWORLD

RUNE

RED BRIDE

DARKEST DAY

SPANKY

PSYCHOVILLE

DISTURBIA

SOHO BLACK

CALABASH

Graphic Novel

MENZ NSANA

Short Stories

CITY JITTERS

CITY JITTERS TWO

THE BUREAU OF LOST SOULS

SHARPER KNIVES

FLESH WOUNDS

PERSONAL DEMONS

UNCUT

THE DEVIL IN ME

DEMONIZED

FULL DARK HOUSE

Christopher Fowler

BANTAM BOOKS

LONDON • TORONTO • SYDNEY • AUCKLAND • JOHANNESBURG

FULL DARK HOUSE
A BANTAM BOOK : 9780553815528

Originally published in Great Britain by Doubleday,
a division of Transworld Publishers

PRINTING HISTORY
Doubleday edition published 2003
Bantam edition published 2004

5 7 9 10 8 6

Set in 10.5/13pt Sabon by
Falcon Oast Graphic Art Ltd.

Bantam Books are published by Transworld Publishers,
61–63 Uxbridge Road, London W5 5SA,
A Random House Group Company.

Addresses for Random House Group Ltd companies outside the UK
can be found at: www.randomhouse.co.uk
The Random House Group Ltd Reg. No. 954009.

Printed and bound in Great Britain by
Cox & Wyman Ltd, Reading, Berkshire.

The Random House Group Limited supports The Forest Stewardship
Council (FSC), the leading international forest certification organisation.
All our titles that are printed on Greenpeace approved FSC certified paper
carry the FSC logo. Our paper procurement policy can be found at:
www.rbooks.co.uk/environment.

For Bill – scientist, firewatcher, father (1923–2003)

ACKNOWLEDGEMENTS

As far as I can tell, all factual details pertaining to Bryant and May's fateful week in the Blitz are accurate, and any minor errors are my own. Where newspaper reports proved skimpy, I relied on personal interviews and memories, including my father's experiences as a firewatcher. I'd like to thank archivist Graham Cruickshank for showing me the secret world of the Palace Theatre. A special warm thank you goes to my agent Mandy Little on this, our first book together. I'd also like to thank my editor Simon Taylor for his excellent suggestions, and everyone at Transworld for bringing Bryant and May to the public. Thank you, Richard, for tea and patience, and to Jim and Sally for sorting everything out. If you'd like to know more about Bryant and May, you can email me at chris@cfowler.demon.co.uk or see www.christopherfowler.co.uk.

'Ne regarde pas en arrière!
A quinze pas fixe les yeux!
Ami, pense à la terre.
Elle nous attend tous les deux.'
('Don't look back! Fix your gaze five yards ahead!
Friend, think of the earth that waits for both of us.')
Orphée aux enfers – Jacques Offenbach

Little drops of water, little grains of sand,
Lots and lots of buckets, standing close at hand,
Yards and yards of hosepipe ready in the hall –
That's the stuff to give 'em when incendiaries fall!
Children's book, 1940

Holmes Road division saw him standing at the window around four thirty. They made fun of him, just as they always do. He opened the window and told them to bugger off, threw a paperweight at them. I should have stayed with [him].'

'Then we would have lost both of you,' said Longbright. She looked up at the splintered plaster and collapsed brick-work. 'I mean, he can't still be alive.'

'I wouldn't hold out too much hope.'

A tall young man in a yellow nylon jacket came over. Liberty DuCaine was third-generation Caribbean, currently attached to the unit in a forensic team with two young Indian women, the brightest students from their year. Liberty hated his name, but his brother Fraternity, who was also in the force, hated his more. Longbright raised her hand.

'Hey, Liberty. Do they have any idea why—'

'An incendiary device of some kind, compact but very powerful. You can see from here how clean the blast pattern is. Very neat. It destroyed the offices but hasn't even singed the roof of the station.' The boy's impatience to explain his ideas resulted in a staccato manner of speech that May had trouble keeping up with. 'There are some journalists sniffing around, but they won't get anything. You OK?'

'Arthur couldn't have got out in time.'

'I know that. They'll find him, but we're waiting for a JCB to start moving some of the rafters. They haven't picked up anything on the sound detectors and I don't think they will, cos the place came down like a pack of cards. There's not a [l]ot holding these old houses in one piece, see.' Liberty looked [a]way, embarrassed to be causing further discomfort.

[L]ongbright started walking towards the site, but May gently [hel]d her back. 'Let me take you home, Janice,' he offered.

[S]he shrugged aside the proffered hand. 'I'm all right, I just [do]n't think it would end like this. It *is* the end, isn't it?'

[Lon]gbright was already sure of the answer. Arthur Bryant [and] John May were men fashioned by routines and habits.

1

OUT WITH A BANG

It really was a hell of a blast.

The explosion occurred at daybreak on the second Tuesday morning of September, its shock waves rippling through the beer-stained streets of Mornington Crescent. It detonated car alarms, hurled house bricks across the street, blew a chimney stack forty feet into the sky, ruptured the eardrums of several tramps, denuded over two dozen pigeons, catapulted a surprised ginger tom through the window of a kebab shop and fired several roofing tiles into the forehead of the Pope, who was featuring on a poster for condoms opposite the tube station.

As the dissonance pulsed the atmosphere it fractured the city's fragile caul of civilization, recalling another time of London bombs. Then, as now, dust and debris had speckled down through the clear cool air between the buildings, whitening the roads and drifting in the morning sunlight like dandelion seeds. For a split second, the past and the present melted together.

It was a miracle that no one was seriously injured.

Or so it seemed at first.

When Detective Sergeant Janice Longbright received the phone call, her first thought was that she had overslept and missed the start of her shift. Then she remembered that she had just celebrated her retirement from the police force. Years of being woken at odd hours had taught her to focus her attention within three rings of the bedside telephone. Rubbing dreams from her head, she glanced at the clock and listened to the urgent voice in her ear. She rose from the side of her future husband, made her way quietly (as quietly as she could; she was heavy-footed and far from graceful) through the flat, dressed and drove to the offices above Mornington Crescent tube station.

Or rather, she drove to what was left of them, because the North London Peculiar Crimes Unit had, to all intents and purposes, been obliterated. The narrow maze of rooms that had existed in the old Edwardian house above the station was gone, and in its place wavered fragments of burning lath-and-plaster alcoves. The station below was untouched, but nothing remained of the department that had been Longbright's working home.

She made her way between the fire engines, stepping across spit-sprays from snaked hosepipes, and tried to discern the extent of the damage. It was one of those closed-in mornings that would barely bother to grow light. Grey cloud fitted as tightly over the surrounding terraces as a saucepan lid, and the rain that dampened the churning smoke obscured her view. The steel-reinforced door at the entrance to the unit had been blown out. Firemen were picking their way back down the smouldering stairs as she approached. She recognized several of the officers who were taping off the pavement and road beyond, but there was no sign of the unit's most familiar faces.

An ominous coolness crept into the pit of her stomach as she watched the yellow-jacketed salvage team clearing a path through the debris. She dug into the pocket of her overcoat, withdrew her mobile and speed-dialled the first of the two numbers that headed her list. Eight rings, twelve rings, no answer.

Arthur Bryant had no voicemail sys Longbright had ceased encouraging him to r after his 'static surge' experiments had magne of a British Telecom call centre in Rugby. S second number. After six rings, John May's voic leave a message. She was about to reply when she behind her.

'Janice, you're here.' May's black coat empha wide shoulders and made him appear younger than (he was somewhere in his eighties – no one was qu where). His white hair was hidden under a grey wooll Streaks of charcoal smeared his face and hands, as thou was preparing to commit an act of guerrilla warfare.

'John, I was just calling you.' Longbright was relieve see someone she recognized. 'What on earth happened?'

The elderly detective looked shaken but uninjured, thankfully late arrival at the blast scene. 'I have absolutely n idea. The City of London Anti-terrorist Unit has already dis counted political groups. There were no call signs of any sort.' He looked back at the ruined building. 'I left the offic at about ten last night. Arthur wanted to stay on. Arthur . May widened his eyes at the blasted building as if seein for the first time. 'He always says he doesn't need to sle

'You mean he's inside?' asked Longbright.

'I'm afraid so.'

'Are you sure he was still there when you left?'

'No question about it. I rang him when I got h told me he was going to work right through the ni he wasn't tired and wanted to clear the backlog. Y how he is after a big case, he opens a bottle of C and keeps going until dawn. His way of celebrati his age. There was something in his voice . . .'

'What do you mean?'

May shook his head. 'I don't know. As thou to talk to me but changed his mind, that v thing he does on the phone. Some officers

1

OUT WITH A BANG

It really was a hell of a blast.

The explosion occurred at daybreak on the second Tuesday morning of September, its shock waves rippling through the beer-stained streets of Mornington Crescent. It detonated car alarms, hurled house bricks across the street, blew a chimney stack forty feet into the sky, ruptured the eardrums of several tramps, denuded over two dozen pigeons, catapulted a surprised ginger tom through the window of a kebab shop and fired several roofing tiles into the forehead of the Pope, who was featuring on a poster for condoms opposite the tube station.

As the dissonance pulsed the atmosphere it fractured the city's fragile caul of civilization, recalling another time of London bombs. Then, as now, dust and debris had speckled down through the clear cool air between the buildings, whitening the roads and drifting in the morning sunlight like dandelion seeds. For a split second, the past and the present melted together.

It was a miracle that no one was seriously injured.

Or so it seemed at first.

When Detective Sergeant Janice Longbright received the phone call, her first thought was that she had overslept and missed the start of her shift. Then she remembered that she had just celebrated her retirement from the police force. Years of being woken at odd hours had taught her to focus her attention within three rings of the bedside telephone. Rubbing dreams from her head, she glanced at the clock and listened to the urgent voice in her ear. She rose from the side of her future husband, made her way quietly (as quietly as she could; she was heavy-footed and far from graceful) through the flat, dressed and drove to the offices above Mornington Crescent tube station.

Or rather, she drove to what was left of them, because the North London Peculiar Crimes Unit had, to all intents and purposes, been obliterated. The narrow maze of rooms that had existed in the old Edwardian house above the station was gone, and in its place wavered fragments of burning lath-and-plaster alcoves. The station below was untouched, but nothing remained of the department that had been Longbright's working home.

She made her way between the fire engines, stepping across spit-sprays from snaked hosepipes, and tried to discern the extent of the damage. It was one of those closed-in mornings that would barely bother to grow light. Grey cloud fitted as tightly over the surrounding terraces as a saucepan lid, and the rain that dampened the churning smoke obscured her view. The steel-reinforced door at the entrance to the unit had been blown out. Firemen were picking their way back down the smouldering stairs as she approached. She recognized several of the officers who were taping off the pavement and road beyond, but there was no sign of the unit's most familiar faces.

An ominous coolness crept into the pit of her stomach as she watched the yellow-jacketed salvage team clearing a path through the debris. She dug into the pocket of her overcoat, withdrew her mobile and speed-dialled the first of the two numbers that headed her list. Eight rings, twelve rings, no answer.

Arthur Bryant had no voicemail system at home. Longbright had ceased encouraging him to record messages after his 'static surge' experiments had magnetized the staff of a British Telecom call centre in Rugby. She tried the second number. After six rings, John May's voice told her to leave a message. She was about to reply when she heard him behind her.

'Janice, you're here.' May's black coat emphasized his wide shoulders and made him appear younger than his age (he was somewhere in his eighties – no one was quite sure where). His white hair was hidden under a grey woollen hat. Streaks of charcoal smeared his face and hands, as though he was preparing to commit an act of guerrilla warfare.

'John, I was just calling you.' Longbright was relieved to see someone she recognized. 'What on earth happened?'

The elderly detective looked shaken but uninjured, a thankfully late arrival at the blast scene. 'I have absolutely no idea. The City of London Anti-terrorist Unit has already discounted political groups. There were no call signs of any sort.' He looked back at the ruined building. 'I left the office at about ten last night. Arthur wanted to stay on. Arthur . . .' May widened his eyes at the blasted building as if seeing it for the first time. 'He always says he doesn't need to sleep.'

'You mean he's inside?' asked Longbright.

'I'm afraid so.'

'Are you sure he was still there when you left?'

'No question about it. I rang him when I got home. He told me he was going to work right through the night. Said he wasn't tired and wanted to clear the backlog. You know how he is after a big case, he opens a bottle of Courvoisier and keeps going until dawn. His way of celebrating. Mad at his age. There was something in his voice . . .'

'What do you mean?'

May shook his head. 'I don't know. As though he wanted to talk to me but changed his mind, that weird hesitation thing he does on the phone. Some officers in an ARV from

13

the Holmes Road division saw him standing at the window at around four thirty. They made fun of him, just as they always do. He opened the window and told them to bugger off, threw a paperweight at them. I should have stayed with him.'

'Then we would have lost both of you,' said Longbright. She looked up at the splintered plaster and collapsed brickwork. 'I mean, he can't still be alive.'

'I wouldn't hold out too much hope.'

A tall young man in a yellow nylon jacket came over. Liberty DuCaine was third-generation Caribbean, currently attached to the unit in a forensic team with two young Indian women, the brightest students from their year. Liberty hated his name, but his brother Fraternity, who was also in the force, hated his more. Longbright raised her hand.

'Hey, Liberty. Do they have any idea why—'

'An incendiary device of some kind, compact but very powerful. You can see from here how clean the blast pattern is. Very neat. It destroyed the offices but hasn't even singed the roof of the station.' The boy's impatience to explain his ideas resulted in a staccato manner of speech that May had trouble keeping up with. 'There are some journalists sniffing around, but they won't get anything. You OK?'

'Arthur couldn't have got out in time.'

'I know that. They'll find him, but we're waiting for a JCB to start moving some of the rafters. They haven't picked up anything on the sound detectors and I don't think they will, 'cos the place came down like a pack of cards. There's not a lot holding these old houses in one piece, see.' Liberty looked away, embarrassed to be causing further discomfort.

Longbright started walking towards the site, but May gently held her back. 'Let me take you home, Janice,' he offered.

She shrugged aside the proffered hand. 'I'm all right, I just didn't think it would end like this. It *is* the end, isn't it?' Longbright was already sure of the answer. Arthur Bryant and John May were men fashioned by routines and habits.

14